THE ARRANGEMENT

Vol. 14

H.M. Ward

www.SexyAwesomeBooks.com

H.M. Ward Press

COPYRIGHT

H.M. WARD PRESS

First Edition: Feb 2014

ISBN: 978-1630350192

The Arrangement

Vol. 14

CHAPTER 1

My head feels like a balloon, swollen and light. I'm lying on my back, inside the box, as my mind screams hysterically for freedom. I blink over and over again, trying to focus, but there's only darkness. I can still move, but it's like my limbs are dead weight. Whatever they injected is making me woozy, but it hasn't taken full effect yet. I can feel it trying to pull me under as each moment passes.

The box tips forward a little and I know we're in the stairwell.

I'm still coherent enough to think and I'm so far past irate that I'm ready to claw someone's face off. Screw that. I am not dying in a box. And Sean. What the holy fuck did he do?

My brain tries to race through scenarios at a sluggish pace and I know I can't wait anymore. We're on a landing. I react, and slam my body into the side of the box. The sudden movement makes the container tip and slip from their grasp. I hit the floor hard, but they didn't think to seal me in. The box falls open on its side and I scurry out. Gabe is cursing and stuck in the corner on the other side of the container. The other thug fell down the next flight of stairs.

Move, I scold myself, and start crawling up the stairs.

Gabe warns, "Don't do it." But I don't listen. He doesn't chase after me. Instead, he goes to help the other man.

I manage to stumble back to my room. Asia sees my zombie-like steps and laughs. "You're a little too toasted to be walking around. You want help?" I try to tell her no, but she thinks I'm high and insists on taking me back to my room.

"I'm fine."

"No, you're not." She's laughing lightly and takes my arm, helping me down the hall. Everything is spinning and tipping. I'm so going to puke. Asia's been talking and her questions finally register. "And she hasn't been in class either. Do you know where Mel is? I'm worried."

"She's been around," I lie. "I saw her last night."

"Ah, so this means Mel has some goodies again. No wonder why she didn't come back. She didn't want to share." Asia makes no sense, and when she's by my door, she reaches for the knob. I have no idea what Black and Sean are doing, but I'm worried they're going to shoot her.

Ripping my arm away from hers, I snap, "You're such a bitch, Asia. Mel didn't come home because she can't stand you. Damn, take a fucking hint."

Asia straightens and holds her shoulders back. Her jaw drops as I speak and then snaps shut. She twirls on her heel and marches back down the hall to her room and slams the door. I feel bad for saying it, but I don't want her involved. I may regret it when I can think straight, but I can barely string together thoughts, much less come up with creative lies.

I know I have seconds before Gabe and his buddy drag me away, so I shoulder my way through the door. Sean is standing in front of Black with fury in his eyes. Black glances over her shoulder at me. Her slender arms are folded over her chest and she looks pissed.

I have trouble controlling my speed and hurl my body right at her, knocking her down. Miss Black hits the floor with an *oof*. I manage to stay on my feet, and stagger over to confront Sean. For half a second I just stare at him, and then I make a fist. Before I know it, my knuckles have connected with his jaw. Sean's face whips to the side on impact and a little trail of red drips from his lip. His blue gaze is on fire and I'm afraid.

I go to punch him again but he catches my hand. I try to pull it away, but he won't let go. "I told you to go with them." He growls the words like a feral animal.

Ignoring him, I yell in his face. "You're engaged to someone else! What the fuck! You lied to me, this whole time you've been lying to me! I want to know why." Black gets to her feet behind me and makes a horrible sound as she grinds her teeth. I'm pretty sure they're going take me to the woods and bury me in that box.

Sean's gaze is locked on mine. "Avery, you have to leave. Now."

"No!" I shove his chest. Black tries to touch my shoulder to spin me around, but I hiss at her, "Don't you touch me!" Miss Black gnashes her teeth, but she backs up after glancing at Sean. I turn to Sean once more and say the words that are burning a hole in my tongue, "Here, you fucker. Take your goddamn ring back and never talk to me again. Ever." I rip my ring off my finger and throw it at his face.

By the time I turn around, Gabe is behind me. His accomplice is pissed and bloody. I'm still fighting the drugs that are trying to pull me under, but I won't let them win. I stagger when the rush of energy slips away and Gabe grabs my arm. "Why don't you listen?" he asks softly.

Sean hasn't moved, offered an explanation or anything. He remains rigid and lifeless. The man is made of stone and I gave him my heart. I let out a pathetic sobbing sound and slump in Gabe's grip before Black says, "Take her out of here. Now."

CHAPTER 2

I'm hauled away and shoved into a car. They abandoned the box. I have no idea where it went. It wasn't in the stairwell when they carried me out. Whatever they shot into my arm makes my eyelids feel like they weight a million pounds. They keep trying to close, but I force them open again.

Time is screwy. I don't know how much has passed or what's going on, but I recognize the building in the city. It's early in the morning by the time we get there. We head up to Miss Black's office, where I'm told to wait until she comes back.

When the other man leaves, Gabe points to a chaise in the corner. "Go lay down."

"No." My arms are folded over my chest. I'm sitting in a chair, staring straight ahead.

"If you were my kid, I'd slap you."

"Oh, please. If I was your kid, I wouldn't be here. You would have killed every single one of them for looking at me funny. Let's not play games anymore, old man. Why am I here?" I can see him shake his head out of the corner of my eye, but he doesn't speak. "I'm dead, right?" I ask because I have to. My heart slaps into my ribs once and then goes back to its slow, drugged beating.

"Avery, listen to me. You've got no friends, no backup, no nothing. The only person batting for you on this team is me, and you don't pay attention." Sighing, he grips his forehead like he has a massive headache. When he glances up at me, his voice is softer. "Listen for once in your goddamn life, and listen closely. Black is full of shit. Watch what she says. Don't take her word over Ferro's. They're both liars, but one of them is two steps ahead of the other."

I'm still too out of it to grasp what he's saying. "What are they doing? And which one is two steps ahead?" I turn and look at him.

"I don't know, but the playing board is much bigger than you think." Gabe disappears without further explanation.

I never felt so stupid in my entire life. I can barely think with this stuff in my veins and I wish that I'd never met Black. My life has totally fallen apart. I'm chasing a mental man that I can never have. No matter what I do, Sean will always be haunted by the memories that hide behind those beautiful eyes. Black is equally ruthless and scares the shit out of me. I have no doubt that she chopped up other girls who gave her trouble and planted them like daisies at the arboretum.

I need to get out of here, but I have nowhere to go—no one to hide me. Gabe is right. I'm alone. I bury my face in my hands and let out a rush of air. I'm fucked. How do I get out of this?

At that moment, Black walks in the room. She slams the door shut and tosses her purse on the desk, nearly hitting me in the head, before sitting down in her chair.

"Do you have an idea what you've put me through?"

"You're not my mother, so don't pretend to care." I glance up at her slowly. My words are sharp, but steady. My speech doesn't slur the way I expect it to. The buzz seems to be wearing off.

Miss Black's red lips curl into a sneer. "I don't care in the slightest what trauma you've been through and if you ever equate me to your mother again, I'll make you beg for death." Her eyes narrow as she speaks and I know without any doubt that she hates me. "The only thing I care about is this company and your little stunt at the hotel put it in jeopardy. Where is Mel?" Staring her in the eye, I shrug. "Fine. You want to play it this way, then we'll play."

Black grabs a pair of sewing sheers from her desk. They're silver with long blades. She stands and walks around behind me. Before I know what she's doing, the crazy-ass woman slices open the back of my shirt. It falls forward and tumbles into a lump in my lap. "There are only so many things to cut before we get to skin, and from the looks of it, you already have a scar. Why add more?"

I'm ready to start a hysterical rant, but I shove it down. I need to be able to think. Miss Black is all about logic. I decide to give her the information she wants. "Mel is fine. She's hiding. The last time I saw her was last night on Long Island. She's not coming back until they find out who killed the look-a-like in Mr. Ferro's hotel room."

She laughs lightly. "Ah, are we back to formalities with Sean? Very well. It's all for the best, because you couldn't marry him and work for me."

"I don't want to work for you." I sound rather dignified for someone sitting in a bra and jeans.

She smiles and slips up onto her desk, and crosses her legs. "Ah, that's where you're wrong. I have a new job for you, one you'll adore. And since you've taken your previous career plans and sent them straight to Hell, I thought this would interest you."

I glance up at her. "Nothing you can say will interest me. I'm done. I'm walking away from this. I didn't see anything and I won't say anything. There haven't been any cops following me and nothing from the night at the hotel points back to you."

"Ah, so they didn't find a bracelet. Funny, because I thought they did." Miss Black smirks. "Avery, my dear, you're not going anywhere, not for a while. And like the rest of the girls, you work when I tell you to."

"No, not me. I'm done."

"So, tell me—where are you going to live? How are you going to pay for food? What about your bills? Do you have a secret trust fund that I'm unaware of, or do you really think you can make it on your own working at the steak house? Because that life wasn't one you wanted, if I recall correctly. This is easy money, Avery. There's a nice house with manicured grounds, a pool, and then there's the money, but you don't need that."

Black slides off the desk and walks to her closet and continues talking. "Ideals won't feed you and keep the rain off your back. They don't protect you either, and like it or not, men want you. You have something that makes them come back for more, over and over again. It took me a while to see that I have you in the wrong position."

I turn in my seat, holding my wadded, torn shirt in my hand. I'm so tired that I can't think straight. For once, I just want to lay down and be left alone. Black's words sound like noise in my ears. "What are you talking about?" I shouldn't ask. I know I shouldn't, but I'm screwed. I'm screwed and I know it. Graduation will come and go and I'll get kicked out on my ass. I'll be homeless.

Unless, I go beg Marty for a bed, and god knows how awkward that would be since he has a mad crush on me. I could share his bed and camp out over there when I thought he was gay, but not anymore. Too many things have happened, but I still yearn for his friendship. What the hell does that mean? I seem to only attract guys that suck. They lie to my face over and over again, and yet I can't let them go. I'm too afraid to let anyone go. It feels like my life has shattered, the shards have been crushed to dust and are blowing away. I can't stand it anymore.

"It's not a complicated notion, Avery. As much as I detest you, there is something about you. Add in that desperation to survive and the job is perfect for you."

"Again, what are you talking about?"

She smiles kindly and the floor of my stomach goes into a freefall. I shouldn't have asked. The back of my neck prickles, as if whatever she's going to say will change my life. "I was like you once—alone and desperate—forced to do things that I didn't want to do." She leans back in her chair and steeples her fingers. "Then I became a madam and my entire world changed. My employer made me the offer once, just as I'm doing for you. Do you understand what I'm offering?"

I stare at her. This is unreal. It can't be happening. All I can manage is, "What?"

Black stares back, her dark eyes utterly unsympathetic. "You heard me."

I have no idea what to say. After a few moments, I lick my lips and say, "Let me get this right. You kidnapped me and brought me here to ask me to take your place?" My voice has a have-you-lost-your-mind tone.

Black laughs lightly and it sends a chill down my spine. "No one can take my place, but I've realized I'm not utilizing your skill set in the best way possible. You'd be a madam in the location where I install you. You still answer to me, but you no longer earn your living laying on your back. Other women will do that and you'll be in charge of them."

I laugh, because I think she's joking. "Yeah, right. Very funny. When are you going to shoot me and dump my body at Captree? This is getting old." I'm tempting her to shoot me. Maybe it's not my brightest move, but I'm too exhausted to think.

Miss Black pinches the bridge of her nose and sighs, before pressing a button under her desk. A moment later, Gabe opens the door. "Yes?"

"Miss Stanz requested that her body be dumped at Captree after her disposal."

Gabe's wrinkled face turns white, but his old eyes remain lifeless. He nods, saying, "Yes ma'am."

She asks Gabe, "Or would you rather have the previous job I mentioned?"

Gabe's expression is stern. "The previous job, Miss Black."

"So convince you're annoying friend to take it and thank me." Miss Black gets up and leaves the room, as if she can't stand the sight of me.

Gabe lets out a rush of air after the door closes behind her. His shoulders lose a little bit of tension as he lowers his huge body into the chair next to mine. "You told her no?"

"Gabe, she wasn't serious. She hates my guts. Why would she offer me something like that?"

"Because that's what she does. Black's business touches this country from coast to coast. Periodically a girl comes along that has that added appeal—like you—where guys can't get enough of them. Then, BINGO, she's found her needle in the haystack. The other women jumped at the chance, and you..." he shakes his head before lowering it in his hands.

I can't take it. Turning toward him, I grab his arm and tug his hands off his face. He looks up at me with those silvery eyes. "Gabe, tell me what the hell is going on. I can't stand this. Someone is trying to kill me and Black is talking jobs? Has she lost her goddamn mind?" I'm practically screaming by the time I finish speaking.

"Shh," he snaps and tugs my arm, so my ear is closer to him. "Don't think you're not expendable to her, because you are—job offer or not. All this shit isn't what you think and I'm not the person that should tell you. Ask Ferro. Ask Black, but not me."

"No, you tell me. Why'd you take me from Sean?"

"I told him to clue you in. He obviously didn't. Ferro didn't want you to be there when the killer shows up. They had to make sure the person saw you go into the room and know that you were there, so we couldn't let them see you leave. That's why we tossed you in that box, or tried to. The entire plan was probably shot to hell, because we had to carry you out when you pitched a fit."

I glare at him. "You stuffed me into a box."

"Touché."

I make an annoyed sound. "Gabe, this makes no sense. So Sean is working with Black?"

Gabe laughs like that was the stupidest thing he's ever heard. "Nah, Black is the lesser of two evils. Ferro didn't want you in the room. He's protective of you and the only person who could keep you safe is Black. Ferro can no longer trust his staff, so he's fucked. He asked Black to keep an eye on you. I seriously doubt he knows what she wants from you. Black has her own agendas and some of them clash with Ferro's."

"So, I'm safe?" Gabe nods. His confirmation releases a slew of emotions that I'd been holding under lock and key. They bubble up and I start shaking before clutching his arm. "I thought he turned on me. I thought you guys were going to—"

Gabe doesn't let me fall apart. "Pull yourself together. Don't drop your guard, kid. We still don't know who is trying to take you out or why. Ferro and Black have been discussing it, and I don't have any theories either. The best they've come up with is that it's someone trying to get even with Ferro."

"Like Henry Thomas?"

"Exactly like Thomas. But Ferro has too many enemies. We can't track all of them and Black is saying its Ferro's problem, not hers. They agreed on a temporary truce so Ferro could take care of the problem and keep you safe."

"Except the killer never showed." Sean is standing in the door. There are bags under his eyes like he's not slept in days. His dark hair is a mess and his jaw is covered in stubble. Sean walks in without looking at me and sits on Black's desk before addressing Gabe, "Out."

CHAPTER 3

After Gabe grudgingly leaves, we're alone. I straighten in my seat. I want to kill him. After everything we've been through, he still doesn't trust me enough to share his plans. While working my jaw, I glance at my nails and say, "So, you're an asshole."

"Possibly." Sean's voice is deep and firm. I hate it when he sounds like this. "My plans got botched when that box showed up early. I was going to tell you." Sean's hands are folded in his lap like this is a normal thing for him. He's acting like he's at a friggin' business meeting.

I want to write him off and tell him to go fuck himself, but I say something else. "Uh huh, and what about the other fiancée? Did you guys pick a wedding date yet or were we supposed to have a double wedding that no one bothered to tell me about?" Lifting my gaze, I continue, "Because I'd be fine with that as long as I'm the first wife. After all, I'm only after you for your money. I have no emotional investment in our relationship at all." My tone dips deathly low as my voice picks up a bitterness that is so jaded it alarms me, but I don't care.

Sean reaches into his pocket and pulls out the engagement ring. When he holds it out to me he says, "Put it back on."

"Bite me."

"I'd love to." The corner of his mouth twitches like he wants to smile—or win—I can't tell what's motivating him.

"I hate you."

"I seriously doubt you've lost all affection for me. It was a calculated risk—one that I had to take. You couldn't be there." His eyes are cold and unapologetic. He watches me, taking in my minor movements, and the way I sit. He's gauging me and soaking up every ounce of detail like a sponge. I wish I could be as unreadable as Sean, but it's not my thing.

My thing is crazy, so I pull it out and let him have it. "Bullshit! What makes you think I'm safer with Black? She could have killed me before you even figured out what happened. Just because you and Black seem to have had a thing doesn't mean you can trust her."

Sean's eyes dip to my bra for the first time since he walked into the room. "Her work?"

"No, I sliced my own shirt for fun. Everyone's going to be dressing like this tomorrow." I roll my eyes and clench my jaw tight to stop the tidal wave of words that I want to accost him with.

"Avery, Black is powerful and if she wants to keep you alive, you'll stay that way. She doesn't invest time or money in perishables."

"Nice."

"It's the truth." His tone is flat. He doesn't plead with me or beg me to listen—he expects me to curse him out and tell him to take a hike. There's fear behind those blue eyes, but that isn't what I want.

"Since when do you care about the truth?" Sean starts to open his mouth to respond, but I cut him off. "No, seriously, I want to know. Was it before or after you fucked me in the box?"

Something changes as soon as the words tumble out of my mouth. Sean's larger-than-life presence fades. For a moment none of his worries are hidden and every single one is displayed on his face. His lips part and it feels like a cheap shot.

"Avery." When he speaks, my name sounds like a warning more than anything else.

"Sean." I mimic, not heeding his warning. "Seriously. You're engaged to someone else. Explain that away. Tell me why it never came up, or why she's living in your goddamn house while you screw me in hotels on the other side of the country! Is she blonde with huge boobs? Did you buy them for her? Is she tall and perfect? Does she satisfy you the way I do? Probably not, right?" Fury burns bright in Sean's eyes as my questions come hurling forth, but it's the last one that makes him angry. "Or do you just keep her around because she looks like Amanda?"

Without warning, Sean slips off the desk and is in my face. Rage engulfs his beautiful features distorting him into someone unrecognizable. His voice sounds more like an animal than a man. "Never say her name again."

My heart pounds hard and fast. He's furious and he should be, but I won't back down. Tears prick the corners of my eyes as her name falls off my lips. "Amanda Ferro."

For a second nothing happens. Our gazes are both narrow and locked, but then Sean starts shaking. I press myself back into the seat as far as I can go, to try and put space between us, but there isn't any. Sean's nose is touching mine and his hot, angry breath slides over my cheeks. For a moment I think he's going to hit me. His jaw works from side to side like he wants to scream at me, but he can't find the right words. Both of his hands are clutching the couch behind my head and crushing it. If he moves, my slender throat will be caught in his vice-like grip and he'll break my neck.

I don't look away. I don't breathe. For a second, time has stopped and I feel horrible. Remorse swells inside of me and before I can tell him that I don't want things like this, he cracks.

Sean Ferro breaks.

He screams and spins around quickly, so that I can't see his face. His shoulders tense further before they shake. I sit up a little and listen. Sean tries to control his breathing, but he can't. Jagged breaths choke him, and it isn't until he turns around that I see what's happened. His eyes are glassy and there's a devastated smile on his beautiful mouth. "I told you that I don't know how to do this, and that isn't an excuse. It's the truth. For years I've been completely isolated and it had to be that way. Then I met you and I'm fucked, Avery. Every time I drop my defenses, you're the one who gets hurt. I can't let that happen. I can't be the man you want me to be. Too many things have happened and no matter what I do, there's no way to change my past."

"I don't want to change you." My words are so soft that I can barely hear them.

"Yes, you do. You want me to be someone I'm not. I'm a loner and I like it that way."

"Sean Ferro, you're lying to yourself. If that were true, why would you be here with me now?" I haven't forgiven him but I'm not going to push him off his mental cliff. I shiver and Sean peels off his jacket and tosses it to me. I pull it on and wrap my arms around my middle. "Thanks."

He nods. "So what now?"

"That's a good question. What do you want?"

"The same thing I've always wanted— you."

I smile sadly and shake my head. "Those are nice words, but the other fiancée will be pissed when she finds out about me. Maybe things are better this way."

"Avery." He tries to cut me off, but I don't let him because it's too hard to say and once I start I can't stop.

Tears roll down my cheeks, one and then the other. I wipe them away with the back of my hand. "No, I'm serious. Maybe you and I are supposed to be friends. Maybe we're supposed to be nothing at all. Sometimes a person shows up when you need them most and disappears from your life. Maybe that guy is you. I needed you Sean and now—"

"Avery," Sean takes a hold of my shoulders and crouches in front of me. "I'm not marrying someone else. And if you say that you don't need me...don't say it. Not right now." His voice picks up a quiver as he finishes speaking.

"You don't have to sugar coat things for me."

"I'm not. Listen to me. I was trying to tell you and I thought I had more time, but then Black showed up and blurted it out. I gave a ring to someone because my publicist said it would make people think I was more approachable. She has a rock on her finger and lives in one of my houses, but I'm never there. Things aren't like that with her. Jamie is actually an employee. She's on payroll, Avery." I'm shaking my head as he's speaking, but he keeps going. "Call her. Tell her who you are. Ask her if you should marry me." Sean hands me his phone and before I can say no, it's already dialing.

A high-pitched voice answer, "Good morning, Mr. Ferro. How can I help you today?" She sounds like a secretary.

Sean nods once, but I can't form words, so he says, "Jamie, please tell Avery the status of our relationship. Don't leave anything out and use as many details as you like. Don't hold anything back." Sean hands me the phone again.

I press it to my ear and listen to this woman repeat Sean's story, but from her side of things. "I was so lucky. Mr. Ferro paid off my student loans and said I just needed to go to dinner with him when he was in town. People were mean to me at first, but money talks. Sean gave me a spending account and told me to walk around, shop, and dine, and tell people who I was. It was part of an attempt to sway the public opinion of him. You see, I do a lot of charity work. I love it and I always wanted to work for a non-profit, but there was no way to pay back my loans. Mr. Ferro made that possible and I don't care what the papers say, he's not a monster. The man's been through a lot. So what if he doesn't wear his heart on his sleeve, you know?"

"Yeah, I know." My chest is so tight that I can hardly breathe. "So it's a charade?"

"Exactly. Our relationship is one hundred percent business and always has been. I don't know if you've noticed this or not, but he has a type—brunettes with brains. I tease him because I'm a redhead and occasionally act a little too blonde for his liking." She laughs lightly. "There's nothing between us, Avery. It's all a show and always has been."

I don't know what else to say. She seems genuine, and what's even more shocking is she seems to care about Sean, like they're friends. Looking at the carpet, I say, "Thank you for talking to me."

"Sure! Call any time." The line goes dead and I hand Sean his phone.

For a second I feel horrible, but it fades. I'm still angry with him. "Come clean, here and now. Everything. Dump it on the table and let's see if we can pick up the pieces."

Sean nods solemnly. "All right, but not here."

At that moment, Black walks in and takes in the scene. There's a ton of tension and I'm standing in front of Sean, wearing his leather jacket, looking up into his beautiful face. She rolls her eyes and sighs dramatically. "Well, Avery, let's have your answer."

Miss Black smirks at Sean after she's seated behind her desk. A dark eyebrow lifts when Black takes in Sean's confusion, and her ruby lips spread into a smile. "Didn't she tell you? I offered to make her a madam."

CHAPTER 4

Sean just stares at me and then stares at Black. "We had an agreement."

"This doesn't violate our arrangement in the slightest. She'll still live in New York, but her occupation will be somewhat different. If you two are no longer engaged, I don't see how it concerns you anyway." Miss Black thinks she's won. The confidence in her gaze says as much. Tapping her fingertips together, she looks over at me.

As I stare at Black, things click into place. She's been telling lies, but they're always seeded with truth. Sean is engaged to someone else, and he is, but the woman is an employee. This entire time Black has been trying to get me to turn on Sean. For a second, I think about screaming at her, but it's better if she underestimates me, so I play along. "What happens if I say no?"

Miss Black drops her hands and sits straight up. "That wouldn't be a prudent move."

I laugh. "Nothing about this job is prudent, and the one you're offering is even worse on the moral scale of life."

"You already broke the scale when you took money for fucking Mr. Ferro, so I doubt that's a sincere concern. What you should be asking is, 'what happens if I say yes?'"

Folding my arms across my chest, I tug Sean's supple jacket tighter. "If I say yes, you have an easy out when the police come looking for the owner of that bracelet. If it leads back here and you're gone, they're going to blame me for the dead girl in Sean's room. I may look stupid, but believe me, I'm not."

Sean moves behind me and sits down so that only Black and I are standing. He's fuming, but he doesn't speak. This is my mess and he lets me fight my battle.

Miss Black's lips curl into an amused grin. "I think you're juvenile and naïve, but not lacking in intelligence. The bracelet in the hotel room wasn't your friend's. It belonged to the dead girl. I sent her over to check on things and something went wrong. No one will track that bracelet back here, and if they do, we're all screwed anyway. Although I try to leave no trails that point back here, there are still signs."

I need more time to process the information. This is news to me. "And if I say yes?"

She grins broadly. "Then you will become my protégé and make more money than you ever thought possible. You'll own Long Island because every politician and bureaucrat will come calling, and when they do, you'll have them by the balls. It's a pretty place to be, Avery. And with the girl-next-door charm you have, combined with the can-do attitude, you'll own Nassau and Suffolk County. You'll never have to worry about money again. You'll always have a roof over your head and it doesn't matter that your parents left you destitute."

The comment about my parents slices through me and leaves my jaw hanging open. It feels like she sucker-punched me in the stomach. There's no air. My parents didn't leave willingly. They did everything they could for me when they were alive, but now they're gone and I'm alone. If things don't work out with Sean, I'm screwed. I have no plan B and everything I've worked so hard for has been torched. My life is comprised of cinders, ash, and tears. And I'm so ready to move on, so desperate to shirk the grief and pain, that her offer sounds tempting.

"Enough." Sean stands and takes my hands, before pulling me toward the door.

"I think she's able to make up her own mind, Mr. Ferro."

Sean glances back at Black. "I know what she's capable of," he smirks, "You're the one who needs to look out."

I pull out of Sean's grip and look back at Black. "I can make up my own mind, Sean. I don't need you to protect me here, and maybe it's not a bad idea. If I say yes, will I have my own bodyguards the way you do?"

Black's smile turns sincere as she nods. "Of course, and Gabe will be one of them. I already know you're comfortable with him."

I nod, and contemplate what she's saying. Sean is standing next to me and looks completely shocked. "You're not seriously considering this?"

"I owe her a freaking fortune, so I can't leave."

"I'll pay it, Avery."

"You can't. It's my mess." I glance over at Black behind her desk. "You paid my medical bills too, didn't you?"

"Of course. I couldn't have collectors examining one of my girls. I added it to your tab. That debt would vanish in a matter of weeks if you took the job I'm offering. And remember, I only offer it once."

The wheels in my head are spinning fast. "Can I take Mel?"

Black smirks. "No, I want you starting over and hiring the kind of woman you are, not more who are like Mel." Because Mel's a dime a dozen is implied by her tone.

"You're wrong about her."

"Regardless, I own her, like I own you. The question is will you continue to work on your back or do you thirst for something more?"

I don't know what to say. Part of me wants to say yes, but the other part wants to take Sean up on his offer to pay off my debt. The truth is, I don't want to owe either of them anything. I need to go look for that buried treasure on Oak Island or something. I'm so screwed. This is a life changing moment, but it's not one I welcome. "I don't—" I don't know what I'm going to say… I just start speaking.

Miss Black lifts her hand and cuts me off. "Don't decide now. One thing at a time. Let's put the person who's trying to shoot you in the ground, and then we can move forward with our business plans."

CHAPTER 5

Sean is silent. We drive east in his little black sports car and neither of us speaks, but I welcome the silence. Once we talk, things will end in one of two ways—we'll be together or we won't. I honestly don't know what I want. This man has darkness in his blood. It's part of who he is and no matter how much I love him, it will always be there. I doubt I can handle that. Having sex in the box made me realize that side of him is still alive and craving domination. No, it's more than that. He wants to own me and control everything I do.

Black's offer is so similar, but so different. If I say yes to her, then she'll control me, but that feels more like a job and the money I make is mine. With Sean, I feel like a moocher. Freeloading isn't my style, but I'm too poor and I've run out of options. Stay with the lying psycho or work for the other lying psycho.

Maybe I should buy a tent with the last of my money and become a hermit. I can camp out at Hecksher Park and steal hotdogs from other campsites. Why do all my plans suck? Before I can even think about it, we pull into the strip club parking lot. Sean cuts the engine and gets out. I kick open my door before he can walk around, and then slam it shut. I follow him to the door.

He knocks loudly. Trystan yanks the metal door open and stands in the doorway. He smirks when he sees Sean. "Need something, Ferro?"

"Not from you, you little shit." Sean tries to shoulder past him, but Trystan won't move.

"Nah ah." He waggles his finger in Sean's face. "Where are your manners? Your mother would be appalled."

"My mother is already appalled, just like yours, except mine didn't run off into the night." Sean says the words lightly, but they sting like acid. I can see it on Trystan's face.

Before the constant smile slips away, Trystan throws a punch. It catches Sean off-guard and connects with his cheek. In a blink, Sean reacts and the two of them are beating the shit out each other in the parking lot while I stand there, ready to collapse. Why do they hate each other? They seriously have so much in common that they could be brothers. Instead, they fight like lunatics.

More punches fly as the swearing and insults grow louder. I stand there with my arms folded over my chest, annoyed. A moment later, Jon is standing next to me. "Ah, what the fuck. They couldn't fight inside?"

I glance at him. "So you're not going to break it up?"

"I've tried before. Once the two of them start, it's hard to pull them apart." Jon sighs and runs his hands through his hair before walking toward the fight and bellowing at them to cut it out. As he predicted, they don't listen.

Mel steps out next to me and glances at them. "Holy fuck. What a buncha stupid white boys. Why don't they just invite the whole fucking police force into the bar? Avery, this has gotta stop. Like now."

I agree and I'm too tired to think. It's cold out here and I'm not wearing a shirt under Sean's jacket. My body aches and is so tired that I'm ready to fall over. I could get Mel and leave, but I need to talk things out with Sean. I don't want to walk around for the rest of my life never knowing what would have happened.

"Fuck it." I'm exhausted and Mel notices. She also notices that I'm not really thinking. I go to the side of the building where there's a spigot and twist it on. There's water, but no hose. That's not going to stop me. I go back to the door and rip off the thick plastic CLOSED sign.

"Uh, Avery…" Mel tries to stop me, but I don't listen. If they want to act like children, then I'm treating them that way.

I twist the faucet until the water is spewing out and then press the piece of plastic against the metal head. It wouldn't work if they were at the other end of the parking lot, but they aren't. All three of them stop when they get blasted with freezing, cold water. Trystan has a cut on his cheek and when it mixes with the water, it runs down his face in a river of red. Sean's temple opened up again and the side of his face is covered in blood. I stand there spraying them as they stare at me and I don't stop until Sean steps away from Trystan.

I'm soaked too. The water sprayed everywhere, soaking me to the bone. When I finally drop the piece of plastic, I say, "I'm going inside, and if you guys have half a brain between you, you'll follow."

Mel is on my heels when I walk through the door. "Holy shit! You're going to get killed by a rock star and two of the Ferro brothers. I can see the headlines now, Poor Little White Girl Never Knew What Hit Her."

"I'm not in the mood, Mel."

"Of course you are!" She's chipper for someone on the run.

"Mel, I need to talk to you. A lot of shit's gone down and I'm exhausted."

Her smile fades. "No problem, Avery girl. Let me find you some dry clothes, or do you just want pants? That bra-only look is so 1980's, by the way."

I forgot. I'm standing there, dripping, with the jacket hanging open. Everyone is staring at me. There are a few girls inside, along with Bryan Ferro. I expect him to tease me, but he doesn't. He scolds Mel, "Hurry up and grab her a sweatshirt. She's freezing." He walks over to me before Sean is inside and the look of concern on his face kills me. This guy who is always laughing and he has no trace of a smile on his face. "How are your stitches holding up?"

"Mine are fine. Thanks."

Bryan glances around quickly and leans in to say something in my ear, something that he doesn't want anyone else to hear. But when Sean comes through the door, and sees us, he practically erupts. Bryan reacts by kissing my cheek and grinning at Sean. "Your fiancé is smokin' hot and freezing. Stop being a jackass for two seconds and take care of her, or I will."

Sean is ready to take Bryan's head off, but his cousin walks away laughing before anything else happens. "Sean." When I say his name the anger melts off his face and he looks down at me. "I ruined your jacket."

"It's okay." Sean runs his fingers through his hair, making water splatter on the floor. "I'm sorry, Avery."

"Don't tell me, tell him." I point at Trystan, who just walked in. He's in the process of stripping his shirt off, revealing ripped abs and a necklace with a ring hanging on it.

Trystan looks up and dabs his wet shirt to his cut. "What?"

Sean's jaw locks tight and I think he's going to lose it, but he doesn't. "I shouldn't have said that, Scott. My apologies."

Jon is standing next to Trystan. His eyes go wide and his chin hits the floor. A second later, Jon and Trystan stare at each other. Then, Trystan smirks and holds up his hands. "If you try to hug me, I'll have to kick your ass again."

Sean tries not to grin. "Asshole."

"Pretty much, yeah."

I jab Sean in the ribs. "You can't apologize to someone and then call them names. What's wrong with you?"

Jon swats his hand through the air and laughs. "We've been trying to figure that out for years. Good luck." Jon and Trystan disappear into the office after locking the front door.

Mel brings me dry clothes, and then Sean and I sneak into the back and find a table. We close the door. I'm afraid and furious. The emotions are battling within me. Sean sits at the little black table. It's covered in nicks and has names carved into the top. It's been repainted with black lacquer over and over again. I don't sit down. I press my finger to the wood and say, "Tell me why I should stay."

Sean's silent for a moment and then replies, "Because I love you. Because you love me."

"And yet, you act like this. You had a business associate kidnap me. They drugged me, Sean!"

"It was the best way to protect you. I'm sorry it didn't work and the fucker is still out there. I won't let him near you, even if you don't want to be together anymore."

I'm so frustrated that I make a noise in the back of my throat and tug at my hair.

"Don't you see? I want to be with you! I want to be your wife and share your life, but you can't seem to grasp the concept of sharing. I don't want to be forced to be someone I'm not. I'm not okay with you hiding things from me, so tell me the truth, and tell me now or this is over." The ultimatum. There, I said it, even though I didn't want to... Things can't go on like this.

Sean takes a long slow breath and lowers his gaze. He stares blankly, and asks, "What do you want to know? Ask and I'll tell you, but realize you may not like the answer."

I slip into my seat opposite him. We don't touch, even though both of us have our hands on the table. I can't look him in the eye, but I manage to get the question out. "How many fiancées have you had, including your late wife?"

"Four."

He's right; I didn't want to hear that. "And I'm the fourth? And the third is a fake, and the first was Amanda. So who was the second?" A sinking feeling fills my chest as I watch him. It's clear that Sean doesn't want to tell me, but he does.

"Your employer, Miss Black." His blue gaze flicks up to meet mine. I gasp when he says it. "And she was the first, not the second."

My lips part in shock. The guy Black mentioned, the one she regretted parting ways with, was Sean? "You dated Black when she was a call girl?"

"Yes, but I had no idea, and when I found out my moral ass couldn't condone her actions, so I left. When I'm in New York, she sets me up with a girl from her company and we act like nothing ever happened between us. I was so young then, barely out of high school, and she was so worried that I'd leave and she'd have nothing. Her fear spawned the reality."

I don't know what to do with this information, so I stuff it in the back corner of my mind. Black mentioned she made a mistake when we first met. There was some guy that she lost because of the job and she seemed to regret it. Was she speaking about Sean? I can't even fathom the notion. She's older than him by at least five years. How'd they even meet?

I switch gears to the other questions I've had rattling around in my mind. "Did you love Amanda?"

He glances up at me. "Did you love your parents?"

My jaw locks and I refuse to show more emotion. My gaze narrows. "I'm not taking anything for granted. Did you love her?"

Sean sighs and runs his hands through his dark hair. "Yeah, I loved her. I wish I was there that night. I wish I died with her so I didn't have to endure this. I'm a morbid fuck, Avery. Seeing you, and finding out you were working for Black, felt like a slap in the face. But, then I realized that you didn't know our history—that you were telling the truth. You captivated me in a way that's incomparable. I had to know more about you. Then, Black put her foot down and said no. I had to twist her arm to get her to say yes for another date. She always says yes to more money. It's the chink in her armor. She's so afraid of being poor again."

"Wait a second—you asked me to marry you knowing that Black would throw a hissy fit?"

"That's an understatement. She's more likely to put a bullet in my brain, but I know she won't hurt you. You're the prize we're fighting over. She wants to keep you around because you're a money tree and I want you because, well, you already know that part."

I swallow hard. I saved the darkest question for last. It's finally time to ask. "And the box?" I don't need to elaborate; we both know what I'm talking about.

His lips are pressed tightly together and he holds his breath. I know he doesn't want to tell me, but he does. "I was angry after Amanda died and handled a call girl a little too roughly in a small space. She was terrified and begged me to stop. I didn't." He doesn't look up. Instead, Sean's gaze is glued to the floor with his hands tugging on the back of his neck, as if he hoping the ground will open up and suck him straight to Hell.

I'm cold, and don't spare him. I have to know what he did and what happened. Being like that with him triggered something. I have to know. "What happened to her?"

Sean's lips are smashed together, forming a thin line. The muscles in his arms are bulging as he pulls on his neck. After a moment he sucks in air and confesses, "I pushed her past her limit. She couldn't stop screaming while I was fucking her, and then she went silent. I thought she was all right, but she wasn't. When I was finished with her, I let her out, but she had a blank expression on her face. I talked to her, but she didn't respond. Her eyes had a vacant haze, as if she was no longer there. The woman is a walking shell of what she'd been. I destroyed her. She's in South Oaks and has been since our encounter."

My eyes are wide with shock. "The mental hospital?" He nods. "And being like that with me, in that small dark space, did what? Made you think of her?" My skin is covered in goose bumps. I want to cry. That woman could have easily been me. I've tried to do that for him, and he reacts to my fear—it arouses him in a way that's incomparable to anything else.

"Yes, I thought of her, and then Amanda. Everything I touch dies in my hand and the same thing's happening to you. You were vibrant when I met you, and now I've blanched the color from your cheeks and caused you nothing but pain."

I say the words that I've been thinking, because that's all that really matters. "How do you want this story to end?"

Sean glances up at me. There's a sheen over those dark eyes and I can tell he's surprised. He expected me to run screaming, but I'm still sitting here. I haven't moved or berated him for his actions. Death can destroy people and make them long to be amongst the ones they lost. I understand that part of him more than he thinks. "I want you to be safe."

I smile sadly at him. "We both know there's no such thing. The concept of safety is fake. We both know that. Anything could happen to anyone at any time."

"You're safer without me. We both know *that*." He sits up straight and shakes his head.

"Perhaps, but if you hadn't come along when you did, I would have done something horrible with someone else to ease my pain. They wouldn't have cared about me. You do."

"Stop making logical arguments, Miss Smith. That's supposed to be my job." He watches me and although I want to smile, I don't. Sean glances away and sighs. "So what now? What do you want, Avery?"

"I know exactly what I want. I want the man that's hidden beneath the layers of grief and scorn. I want to stop feeding the monster that preys on darkness and fear. I want the real you, the one you've banished, because you're afraid that man will turn to dust in the daylight. I want you—the real you. The man that laughs with his whole body, the one that stuffed snow down my pants, and brought me a gourmet dinner on the beach. I want the man who put the ring on my finger and I don't want him to run when he's afraid."

Our gazes lock as I speak, and those last few words cut him, but it's true and he needs to hear it. I say it as gently as I know how, but kid gloves won't help right now. He needs to hear the truth. "Sean, I know you don't think of yourself as a weak person, but with this, you are. Cowering, and disguising who you are and what you think, isn't living—it's hiding."

Sean stands abruptly. His hands tense at his sides and his lungs fill with air quickly, like he wants to scream. But Sean swallows it back down and strides across the room, away from me. Before I can say another word, Sean disappears through the door without looking back.

CHAPTER 6

I remain in the stripper's dressing room until Mel finds me. I'm lying on a bench with my arm over my face. Mel starts chattering the instant she sees me. "That man has some seriously oversized ovaries. Can you say PMS? He barked at anyone and everyone before shoving his way outside."

Moving my arm, I glance at her. "Tell me you're talking about Trystan."

"Hey! Don't you go dissin' my man. Me and Crème Brule are going to be the perfect couple, get married, and have lots of perfect babies. You wait and see." Mel's voice has that teasing tone. She has a serious crush on Trystan, which means she won't go after him. She's like Sean with things like that.

Anyone she actually cares about, she keeps at arm's length—except me.

I sit up and swing my legs to the floor. "Does he know you call him that?"

"What? Like he'd be offended. It's the perfect dessert, all rich and white." She giggles and then slaps her hand over her mouth. "Uh, you didn't see that."

I roll my eyes. "You are so mental. If you like him, ask him out."

"He's a rock star, Avery. You don't just walk up to the guy and say, 'hey, you wanna go out with me?' Plus, Miss Black will kill me."

"Miss Black wants to kill you anyway. And you should do what you want. Life's too short." I feel a dazed look settle on my face—the one I have when my mind starts to wade through dark thoughts. My mind is a goddamn swamp. No matter which direction I turn, there's more dark sludge. It's everywhere.

"So, why'd Mr. Pampered-Ass run?"

I look over at her with a sheepish grin. "I told him he was a coward."

Mel's jaw drops. "Holy shit on toast! You did not!"

"I did. He asked what I wanted and I told him—I want him to stop running from himself."

"Psh, if that's not the blind leading the blind, I don't know what is."

"It is not."

"It is so. You're gonna lead that boy right off a cliff. Avery, you don't even have your own shit together. How can you ask him to do that when you can't?"

I puff up, offended. "I can so!"

"Avery girl, I love you, but you can't see past your tits on this. You cower and hide from life the same way he does. How you choose to manifest that fear is different and more socially acceptable, but you're both in the flame out stage. You're no better than him."

It feels like she punched me in the stomach. I raise my voice and wag a finger in her face. "You don't know shit about this, okay. You don't know Sean or what he's done. We're not the same."

"Yeah, that's where you're wrong. You're both candy-coated crazy people. You seem all sweet on the outside, but once you get past that outer shell, you're both a fucking mess. If you can't admit that, I don't know if we can be friends. It's one of the only things we have in common." She smiles at me. "Avery, you have to know that about yourself. Are you seriously sitting there, telling me that you had no fucking clue?"

Am I really that messed up? I thought I was healing. My hackles lower a little bit and I admit, "It's not intentional."

"Of course not, and that's the point. It's a defense mechanism—you can't turn it off. If you tried, you'd have nothing to shield yourself with. You just told Wonderbread that he's a coward for leaving his defenses up. The man's been through some serious shit."

"And you're defending him…"

"If that's your main issue with the guy, yeah."

"He put some call girl in South Oaks."

"Did he light her on fire or fuck her?" I glance at her like she's crazy. "Uh, Avery, call girls are there to be screwed. If she didn't want him to do her, she shouldn't have taken the job. If he lit her on fire or buried her alive to listen to her scream, then I'd be more concerned."

"He doesn't do that, but he likes fear. He thrives on it."

"Dark fucker, isn't he?" I nod. "Kind of like me. Well, since you two are no longer an item, I want Sean. I bet I can make him cry."

"He'll make you cry and beg for mercy." I know she's teasing, trying to get a rise out of me, but I don't take her bait.

Mel slaps her hands on her jean-clad knees, "Well, if that's all, then I—"

Mel is ready to walk away, but the offer from Black is still bobbing up and down in my thoughts. Every time I consider it, I think it's ridiculous and shove it back down, but it pops up again. I blurt it out before she can finish her sentence. "Black offered to make me madam."

Mel is half standing, with her butt sticking out and her hands still on her knees, when she pauses. Her jaw drops and she sits back down. "White girl say what?"

"Hey, that's my catch phrase."

"Yeah, it didn't sound right coming out of this luscious mouth. But enough of that.

Black seriously offered?" I nod and go into the details. When I finish Mel is uncharacteristically silent. "What'd you say?"

"She told me to think about it."

"Are you going to do it?"

"I don't know." I'm picking at my nails as I speak. "I'm kind of thinking that it depends on what happens with Sean, but then I'm depending on Sean for everything. Black tapped into one of my biggest fears and twisted."

"I'd let you stay with me, but I'm screwed everyway 'til Tuesday until they catch whoever shot my twin."

I blink at her. "She looked like you."

Mel puts her hands on her hips and tips her head to the side. "Yeah, we've been through this already. You saw her, thought she was me…"

My brain is grabbing at strings and my neck prickles. I don't know what it is, but something is off. I can't place my finger on it. "Wait a second." I pull out my phone and call Black.

"What?" she snaps.

"The girl you sent to check on us at the hotel—what'd she look like?"

Black sighs dramatically into the phone. "Avery, I don't have time for your—"

I'm insane and cut her off, saying each word staccato. "What. Did. She. Look. Like?"

Black huffs and spits out a description. "It was Tawny—dark hair with ghastly gold streaks, caucasian with olive skin, green eyes, about five foot seven, and a buck ten."

"And she died?"

"Yes! Avery, we've been over this already." Miss Black is yelling at me, but she's wrong. Her information is totally wrong and she doesn't know. "Unless you have something helpful to add, or you're accepting your new position, I suggest you hang up."

Done. I disconnect and stare at Mel. "There's another dead body."

CHAPTER 7

"What? Who?" Mel's golden eyes go wide.

"The girl that was in the room—the one who looked freakishly like you—wasn't the girl Black sent over. It was someone else. Black assumed the dead call girl was hers. She never saw the body and the police still haven't released her name, but I saw her." I shake my head and shiver. Continuing, I think out loud, "That means the original hooker that Black sent to our room was either in on it or she's dead." I tell Mel what Black told me.

"I know Tawny and that wasn't her. I'm calling her." Mel pulls out her phone and dials. After a second she hangs up. "It went straight to voicemail."

"Her battery is dead."

"Or she's at the bottom of the bay." Mel tenses and presses the edge of the phone to her lips.

"Mel, I don't like this. What if it's just some random person killing off Black's girls? I mean, they tried to take a shot at me, they tried for you, and Tawny's missing." My throat's grown so tight that I can't swallow. "What if this has nothing to do with Sean and everything to do with Black?"

Mel's golden gaze cuts over to me. "I don't trust Black, period. But offering her own staff up to be slaughtered isn't like her. Especially you and me. We're her bread and butter. No one out earned me until you came along."

I add, "Black has a pretty big fear of being poor."

"I can't blame her." Mel rubs her hands over her face and shakes her head. "It makes no fucking sense. Someone is playing us and I'm inclined to think it's one of the fucked up Ferros since all this started when Sean came around."

"It's not him." I say it with complete conviction.

"But how do you know?"

"I just do."

"That's a shitty answer when people are getting whacked, Avery, and you know it."

"It's not Sean." I repeat myself with utter confidence. Standing, I start to pace while rubbing my chin. "Sean has his own stuff going on, and he only fights back when prompted."

"What about that shit with Trystan on the way in?"

"There's bad blood between them."

"But Rockstar didn't start that fight. Your boy did."

"And no one ended up dead in a dumpster either, Mel. Come on, think! What are we missing?"

We're both quiet for a long time. I keep trying to pin this on Naked Guy or Henry Thomas, but something feels off. It's too easy to pin it on one of them and there's no real motive. Well, not one worth killing for. Henry is embarrassed and irate that Sean stole someone he wanted, again. Henry's also pissed that Amanda died, but it doesn't make sense for him to kill me to get back at Sean, not if Henry actually liked me. That's the part that doesn't fit in his puzzle.

Maybe he didn't like you. Maybe he was using you. My inner-voice is a pain in the ass.

Mel huffs and shakes her head, still on the bench. "It makes no sense. We've got someone shooting at you and me. Maybe it's a vendetta against Black?"

"By who?" I turn and look at her. "Who would want to wipe out her staff, because that's what it looks like they're doing. That's why Black wants to protect me and she sure as hell doesn't want anything to happen to you."

Mel makes a sound of disbelief. "She doesn't give a flying fart what happens to me."

Shaking my head, I correct her. "I asked to take you with me, if I accepted the position as a madam. Black said no."

Mel glances up at me with her eyebrows pinched together. "That's weird."

"Not if you're her main girl. I mean she'd want to keep you around."

"Yeah, but she's sending you off. Someone doesn't want us talking to each other. They think we'll figure things out." Mel bites her lip as she thinks.

I lean against the wall and tap my nails on the thick dark paint. "Mel, I don't know how to handle this. If we call the cops, there's nothing to tell them."

"And they'll throw my ass in jail. No cops." Her eyes are wide and frightened.

"So, what can we do?"

"It's simple. This is the way things were on the streets where I grew up. No one saves you, except you. There's no white knight, no police officer that will rescue you. It's time to fight or die, Avery."

I repeat Mel's old words, softly, "Surviving justifies anything."

"Fuck, yeah."

CHAPTER 8

I'm nervous, but I try to shove back the emotions. If I'm a psychotic troll, then I won't notice what's going on. Emotions cloud my judgment and make me second-guess myself. That won't help me now. I have to trust my gut and that's all there is to it. Daddy used to say that the best decisions are the ones you can feel. They have no explanation—you just know.

That's why I find Sean. He's sitting at a table with a half empty bottle of whiskey. I'm exhausted and ready to fall asleep on my feet. When I sit down, I know that I'm going to have trouble getting up again. Sean doesn't acknowledge me, so I speak first. I offer the thing I want, because there's no way to communicate how I feel. I'm mad at him and disappointed, but I don't want to fight anymore.

I reach across the table and touch the back of his hand. "Come to bed with me."

Sean doesn't move. Instead, he stares at my fingers on his. After a moment I withdraw my touch and repeat myself. That's when he finally speaks. "Avery, I can't."

"I need to sleep and so do you."

His eyes flick up. They're filled with so many emotions that I can barely stand to look at him. It's as if the man has been torn in two and is still alive. It's cruel and merciless, washing over him again and again like the waves pounding against the shore. He can't escape his agony. "Not this time."

"I'm not taking no for an answer. We don't have to talk. I just want you near me—we don't have to touch. I know you don't want that right now. Come with me, Sean. Jonathan said there's an office in back with an inflatable bed. He already blew it up for me. Don't make me go alone."

There are sharp words on the tip of his tongue, but he swallows them back. "What do you expect me to do?"

"Sleep."

"No, after that. Tomorrow and the next day. One moment you seem fine with who I am and what I've done, and the next you're calling me a coward." Sean is leaning back in his chair while he rubs the side of his shot glass with this thumb.

"Nothing good comes after 3am and it's so far past that, Sean. We're both exhausted. Let's sleep for a while and talk about it later." My eyelids are lead and I swear to God that my head is going to fall forward and hit the table in a matter of moments. It sways on my shoulders as my lids droop.

"You still trust me?"

"Yes." There's no hesitation, no question about it. I completely trust him. Sean watches me as I put my head on my hand and lean heavily upon it. "Do you trust me?"

The corner of his lips twitches. "That's a silly question."

My elbow starts to slide and my head is going down. I can't stop it. I rest my over-sided, extra heavy melon on my arms as I fold them on top of the table. "I'm a silly girl."

"No, you're not. That's why I'm having so much trouble with you. Avery?"

I hear his voice, but I can't speak any longer. I'm too tired. "Mmmm?"

"Don't leave me."

Turning my head, I open my eyes and smile at him, sleepily. "I'm not going anywhere. You're stuck with me, Mr. Jones." My words turn to a whisper as my eyes close. Sean's voice fills my ears a moment later, but I have no idea what he's saying. When I don't respond, I'm jostled awake as I'm lifted from my chair. When my feet won't move to walk, Sean swears under his breath, and then lifts me into his arms.

He carries me back into the room with the blow-up bed, muttering, "So much for not touching for a while."

CHAPTER 9

My dreams are strange. The drowning nightmare collides with something new. One second I have the watery noose around my neck and the next I'm holding a gun and the walls are bleeding my name. I've shot someone. The pilot. A second after he dies, the man stands. His face is disturbing—it's ghostly pale and rigor has set in, so all his loose flesh is pressed to the side. Crimson overflows from his eyelids, pouring down his chalky cheeks like twin rivers of blood. He moves so slowly, but I feel like I can't escape. The man reaches for my neck and strangles me. Just as I suck in my last breath he explodes. Pieces of flesh fly in every direction and splatter against me. I scream and see Sean standing in blood red smoke. He walks toward me holding a noose. His voice sounds like he's a million miles away even though he's right in front of me. "Everything I touch..."

When his cold fingers press against my cheek, I screech, terrified. Suddenly, I'm in a box and the packaging peanuts are sucked out. The cardboard turns to silk and I realize it's a coffin. I scream until my throat is raw and my lungs burn, but no one saves me.

Mel stands at my graveside, above me, patting her eyes with a tissue. "I tried to tell her, but she wouldn't listen." She's talking to Marty, who says nothing. "Surviving justifies anything."

The inside of the casket turns to fire and as the flames lick my feet, I can't stand it anymore. I scream as I sit upright. I've clawed the satin off the coffin and it's wrapped around me, pinning my arms to my sides. Tears streak my cheeks as I thrash, trying to get out.

That's when I feel hands on my shoulders and hear his voice, "You're all right. Wake up, Avery. Avery...?"

When my eyes open, I'm terrified. Sean is holding my shoulders and watching me. I want to break down and cry. I want to fall into his arms and purge my sorrow until there isn't any left, but I can't. "I'm fine." I snap the words, embarrassed, and pull away from him. The blankets are tangled around my hips and legs.

"I didn't want to wake you, but you were—"

"I'm fine." I repeat the words again, more sternly this time.

"Very well." Sean leans back against the bed. He's still wearing his clothes. I'm in a shirt and no slacks. Getting tangled in the bedding always makes my nightmares worse, but this was the most horrific one I've ever had. I'm sitting on the edge of the bed, facing away from him. "Do you want to talk about it?"

"No."

"All right, then, let's get some food and get out of here for a while."

"Sean," I turn to look back at him, wondering what he wants from me. The room is cold and nasty looking. It's as if it hasn't been cleaned in a decade. Grime covers the walls and paint is old and cracked. There are filing cabinets along the opposite wall and a metal door to lock the employees out. I'm surprised Jon let us in here, especially with the way he and Sean are at each other's throats.

Emptiness consumes me and I shiver. I don't know what to do. I feel so lost. The one place I want to be, I'm not allowed. Sean won't let me touch him.

Sean must read my thoughts because he holds out his arms toward me. "Come here." I do as he says and crawl toward him on the bed. It gives beneath me and I crash into his chest. Sean's strong arms close tightly around me and he kisses the top of my head. "This is where you belong."

I know he doesn't like me against his chest, so it's weird to hear him say it. I hedge, "No one gets this close to your heart for long. I know that. It's all right, Sean. I'm asking too much."

"But maybe you're right. Maybe you should be that close to me. Maybe I should drop my walls a little, at least around you. You trusted me to do things that terrify you because it's what I needed. I can do the same for you. I can hold you. I can let you in."

Tears sting my eyes and I start blinking rapidly, trying to chase them away. "Don't say things like that to me." I push away from him. I can't take any more promises that crumble in my hands. I'm completely mental.

I try to stand and walk away, but Sean grabs my wrist. "I want to be there for you, I swear to God. I just don't know how. Avery, tell me what you need."

I shake my head and turn my face away from him so he can't see the pain in my eyes. I want a man that doesn't need directions. That snappy little voice in my head reminds me, *they all need directions.*

Pressing my lips together, I look back at him. Sean's rumpled clothes cling to his toned body. His arm is extended toward me, barely holding on. It's as if he'll set me free, if I want it. And that's the question I can't answer. What do I want? Do I want this kind of relationship? Do I want to be owned by someone? No matter what he says, that's part of Sean Ferro. Even if I tried to break him of that habit, he'll always feel that way. I'm his. Is that so bad?

My mind shifts and compares him to Black. If I work for her, she'll own me as well. It seems like no matter which path I choose, someone will be making me do things that I don't want to do. I can't picture myself in Black's position at all, but then again, having money and never worrying about where I'm going to live would be nice. It feels more secure than a life with Sean. Sean's mood changes with the breeze. I'm walking eggshells around him. I want to be myself and Black's offering that to me.

Before I can answer, Sean derails my thoughts. He releases my wrist and crawls across the bed and kneels in front of me. He offers an unsure smile. It lights up his face for a second and then fades. "I should give this back to you, if you're leaving." He pulls the ring off his finger and holds it out for me.

Staring at it, I wonder what to do. I want to take it back and I don't. I want to yell at him and I want to hug him. That settles it…that's the test. If he can't do something as simple as a hug, I can't take this anymore. I need to be comforted and I need his arms around me. I go in without warning and wrap my arms around his waist, and press my body firmly to his chest. Sean tenses and his hands hover like he doesn't know what to do. Right when I'm about to pull away, his strong hands come down around me, and hold me tight. Sean presses a kiss to my temple and then does the unthinkable—he rocks backward and pulls me down on top of him.

I yelp and fall onto his chest. He laughs lightly, but doesn't let go. "You have a one track mind, Miss Smith. All you want are hugs, day and night. What's a guy supposed to do? I'm going to have some serious chaffing at this rate." His teasing is light, but there's worry behind his eyes.

I slap his chest and try to pull away, but he won't let me. We're both laughing and a second later I'm staring at his lips, dying to taste them. Sean slips his ring onto a filing cabinet and sweeps his eyes over my body before leaning in slowly. It's like a first kiss. I'm flushed and nervous, hot and excited. I wonder if he's going to do it, if he's really going to taste my lips. Sean said he wouldn't, that he needed time, but the way his gaze dips to my mouth and the way he barely breathes—it makes me think he wants this kiss as badly as I do.

Make up your mind, Avery. You can't keep doing this to yourself. The voice inside my head has a warning tone, like I'm trying to set my eyelashes on fire.

I counter, *He passed the hug test. Shut up!*

Yeah, 'cuz that was a great test.

Dear God, I've gone crazy. I'm talking to myself instead of kissing a really hot guy. One kiss won't hurt anything. I can still decide things later. It doesn't mean anything. Well, it shouldn't, but it does, and this hug means everything to me, too.

Sean's eyes are locked on my mouth and as he inches closer my stomach fills with butterflies. I watch those dark lashes as he gets closer and closer. At some point I stop breathing and only notice when I shiver. Sean lingers kissably close, but doesn't move. "Kiss me, Avery."

I press my lips together firmly and shake my head ever so slightly. "Sean—"

"Kiss me. Use me. Take anything you want. I'm yours. I'll be yours until I take my last breath and think of you every time I see the sky, the sun, or a snowflake. I can't escape you and I don't want to. Say I haven't lost you. Tell me that you still love me."

"I…" I love him. I know I do, but the words stick in my throat. I want to cry, but rather than giving into the emotional basket case side of my persona, I close the distance and press my lips to his. My eyes close as I savor the way his mouth feels against mine, warm and soft. I linger a bit longer than I should and then pull away.

Sean watches me as I sit back on my knees and press my hands to my lap. I'm shaking. I need to put some space between us. I have to think things through. My life hasn't turned out the way I wanted, but there's still an ember of hope that I can turn things around. I push up off the bed and stand. Sean doesn't move. His blue gaze dips as if he knows what I'm going to say.

"I can't. I need to go." I don't explain further. My eyes are glassy and I turn away before tears drip down my cheeks. It feels like someone is squeezing my heart so tight that it can't beat. I need him and that's what scares me most.

CHAPTER 10

I leave Sean in the room alone and try to find Jon. The place is quiet. I don't think he's opened the strip club one night since he bought it. I pull on my shoes, half hopping across the dimly lit room. Right before I wrap my knuckles against the door, a hand lands on my shoulder.

I want it to be Sean, but when I turn around, it's Trystan. "I wouldn't go in there, if I were you."

I nod and avoid his intense gaze. Tucking a piece of hair behind my ear, I explain, "I need a ride."

"And a bodyguard. Is Sean really letting you walk around without one?" Trystan glances back at the room where Sean and I slept with disgust.

"I don't want one. Trystan, I just need a ride." When he doesn't answer, I pull out my cell phone and Google cab companies.

That's when he huffs. His eyes cut to the door and then back to me. "Put that away. I'll take you wherever you need to go."

"You have a car?" I'm asking because I didn't see one in the parking lot.

He smirks. "Yeah, I have a car." A few moments later a huge-ass Hummer pulls up. The windows are tinted as black as the paint. There's an older man driving. He slips out of the vehicle and opens a door.

I punch Trystan's shoulder lightly and laugh. "Nice car. You made it sound like an old clunker."

"I keep that one for personal use." Smirking, Trystan folds his arms over his chest and leans against the vehicle. "So, do you need company? I don't have to be at rehearsal for a few hours."

I glance up into his eyes and can see the concern. He thinks Sean is mistreating me, that these tears are because of him, but they aren't. They're my fault. I'm the one who walked away. "You don't have to do that. I just need some air, you know?"

He nods. The smile fades and he's serious for a moment. Trystan dips his chin toward his chest and looks down at his Chucks. "Do you believe in destiny? Or do you think life is one random event after another?"

I stare at him for a moment. When he looks up at me, I can tell that it's important to him, but I'm not sure what he's wanting to know. He must read it on my face, because he explains. "If it's destiny, it doesn't matter what you do, you'll end up with Ferro. But if we call the shots...sometimes there are no second chances. Sometimes things just don't work, and people say 'it wasn't meant to be,' but that's bullshit, right? You want to start over. I see it in your eyes—but you linger too much in the past. I'm guilty of the same crime. If you're a fate enthusiast, then have it, but if you want things to work out, then there's only one way to do it and running away won't fix that problem."

I tense and snap at him. "A lifetime of shrinks couldn't fix my problems. Don't act like you know me. You have no right."

Trystan lifts his hands palms toward me, as if he meant no harm. "Of course." His smile returns as I climb up into the Hummer. "Tell the driver where you want to go. Hope this isn't good-bye, Call Girl."

I can only nod, because I don't know what this is. My stomach is tied in knots and I can barely swallow. The driver closes the door and I tell him the address before sitting back in the seat. I enjoy the quiet ride until we pull up in front of the apartments.

After the driver opens my door, I hop down. "Will you wait a moment? I'm not sure if he's home."

"Certainly." The old man isn't like Gabe. He's thin as a rail and looks like he might fall over if the wind blows too hard.

I hurry over to the door and knock. Dread fills my stomach, because it's possible that he'll tell me to go away, but I can't. He's one of my best friends and when this all started he didn't condemn me for my new job.

Marty pulls open the door. It's early and overcast. He stands in the doorway with sleep in his eyes and a messy head of sandy hair. There is a pair of plaid boxers hanging low on his trim hips and a loose once-white T-shirt.

"Hey," I say tentatively. When he doesn't answer I add, "I didn't know if I should come—"

Marty gives me one of his signature grins and pulls me into his arms for a quick hug. When he pulls back, he holds both my shoulders. "You're always welcome here."

I wave to the driver to take off and head inside. His apartment is just the way I remember it. The little room has his bed, a kitchen with dirty dishes in the sink, pizza boxes littered across the floor, and his books are everywhere. "Finals just ended. Sorry, the place is wrecked." He rubs his eyes hard and takes a deep breath.

"It's fine."

He looks over at me while he goes to the kitchen. "So, you didn't show up for any of them, did you?" There's a bit of annoyance in his tone, as if he's disappointed with me.

"No, something came up." I don't want to get into the guy trying to kill me, because I can't tell anyone—even Marty—that I killed the pilot. I shiver thinking about it, and shove the thought away. I'm going to go crazy before I'm thirty. I can feel it. I'll be the Long Island madam with forty-two million cats. It'll be pussyland all right. I groan and sit down on a stool.

Marty shoves a bowl of dry cereal at me. "Sorry, no milk. It turned to cottage cheese a week ago. I haven't been shopping yet."

"It's fine." I pick at the sugar covered corn flakes and pop one in my mouth. "How have things been?"

He leans back against the counter and pours some of the cereal into his mouth directly from the box before answering. "Do you mean before or after there was a dead girl at the hotel you were at? Or how you hung up on me mid-call and didn't bother to tell me shit? Because right around then, I was feeling peachy. Just fuckin' peachy, Avery." He slams the box down on the counter and turns his back on me. His hand clutches his temples like he has a massive headache. "I thought you were dead. Mel disappeared, and no one had the decency to tell me jack shit, so of course I'm fine." When he turns back around, Marty glares at me. The look is so cold that I shiver.

I've never heard him curse so much before. It's unnerving coming from him. "I would have called if I could have. Things are out of control and I came here because I wanted your help, but if you're too pissed to—"

Marty's head is tipped to the side and his shoulders are rigid. As soon as I speak, I start for the door, ready to leave. Marty deflates and stops me. Grabbing my wrist, he spins me around. "I was worried about you, that's all."

"And there's a lot to worry about, which is why I'm here."

He nods. It's an acknowledgement that he won't bring up the past few nights or ask about them again. His grip lingers on my wrist. That's when his gaze narrows in on the gash on my arm. I'm wearing a hoodie over my shirt and a pair of jeans. I was cold when I left, so I grabbed it. I think it's Jon's sweatshirt, so it's way too big for me. I pushed the sleeves up to my elbows and he can see the bottom of the wound. "What the hell?"

I tug my arm away from him and push the sleeves down. "Don't." It's a one-word warning that means a million things. Don't say it. Don't push me. Don't ask...just don't.

His jaw tightens and I can tell he wants to scream at me, but he doesn't. "So, what can I do for you, Avery?"

I sneer at him and mutter. "I liked it better when I thought you were gay."

He rolls his eyes before fluttering his lashes at me. "Go on, girlfriend. Tell me what's on your mind and then we can have a bitchfest about men and eat too many donuts." He watches me and finally smiles. His voice goes back to the lower register, without the extra flare. "Seriously, Avery, I'm here for you. I'm just fried. Finals were a bitch and I was really worried about you. It looks like I had every right to be concerned."

"You did. I'm in a bad spot." I go into how Black wants to make me a madam and that I owe her a ton of money. I explain why I don't want Sean to pay the debt and that Black paid my hospital bills. "I'm appalled to say the idea of being a madam isn't horrifying." I'm gripping my hands in my lap, twisting them until they burn.

Marty is sitting on the floor across from me with his back to the wall. "There's only one question to ask yourself—do you want to do it?" I shrug. "It sounds better than being a call girl. How long will it take you to pay back Black if you say yes?"

"I don't know. Not long, I suppose. Much faster than if I kept working as a hooker."

"It sounds like you want the job, so take it."

"It's immoral, Marty!" My jaw drops at how quickly he urges me to take the job.

"Who cares? It'll give you the life you wanted and besides, it's not like you're little miss wholesome right now anyway. You're a whore. A madam is a step up." I gasp when he says those last words. It feels like he's punched me in the stomach. "Avery, don't be like that."

"Like what? Human? Marty!" I make a noise in the back of my throat and jump to my feet. Marty doesn't get up. He sits there with his long legs extended, and crossed at the ankle. I pace back and forth like an elephant, pounding my feet on the floor.

"Avery, it's what you are. You need to be proud of it, otherwise it'll eat away at you until you can't stand to look in the mirror anymore. Does Black have ethical issues with her job? With preying on poor college girls? No, she doesn't. If you want that life, you have to not give a shit. It's money. It's your body. Be proud or quit. You can't be a prude and be a whore. The dichotomy will drive you insane."

I stop pacing and point two fingers at my head. "Hello! What do you think is going on here? I hate this!"

"Then quit. Let Ferro pay your bill and blow him off."

This is why I came here. Marty is so practical that he comes across rather heartless at times. Looking down at him, I finally confess, "Sean proposed."

"So, there are strings on that money. So? Say yes and then leave him."

I shake my head and lean back against the wall, standing next to the spot where

Marty sits. "I don't want to leave him." I slide down the wall until Marty and I are sitting hip to hip.

He's quiet for a while. "Where's your ring?"

"I gave it back."

"Why?"

"Because I don't know what I want. He's dark, Marty. I'm sick of living like that. I've been mourning too long. I spent more time in the graveyard than a Goth kid. I just want to live again, but I don't know how. Sean pulls me backwards."

"I remember you saying the opposite. Actually, I know you said it—he makes you forget your grief and pain. It all fades away when fairy Sean sprinkles his pixie dust on you and graces you with his magical presence." Marty wiggles his fingers when he says pixie dust and uses a mocking voice that sounds a lot like mine.

"I did say that, and with most things it's true."

"But—" he prompts when I don't reply. But, I can't answer. It'd be cruel. The guy has a crush on me and to talk about having sex with another guy is just wrong. Before I can reply, he says, "Ah, the beast with two backs. Yeah, that'll be weird to talk about it."

"English Lit final?"

"Yeah. Shakespeare was a bit of a perv. Anyway, back to your problem—work it out."

"Gee, thanks. Why didn't I think of that?" I roll my eyes as Marty shoulders me.

"You can be such a dumbass, you know that?"

"What? Me?"

"Yes, you. If you don't like the way things are going with freak-o in the sack, tell him. Good lovers are made, not born. If you don't talk about it with him, how is he supposed to know?"

"He does know. I thought it was a good thing to compromise, but I can't keep doing the things he likes." I stare into space remembering the box. I clutch my knees into my chest and hold onto my ankles as tightly as I can. "He scares me sometimes, Marty."

For a long time, no one talks. We just sit there in comfortable silence. Marty finally speaks, "Your husband should be your best friend—he shouldn't scare you. I'm all for you being happy, Avery, but it sounds like he's a dipshit. Actually, I know he is."

I'm biting my upper lip, thinking. "So you think I should take the job with Black and leave Sean?"

He pushes up off the floor. "I think you should do what makes you happy. Out of everyone I know, you deserve happiness the most." He reaches down, extending his hand toward me. "Come on. I'm taking you to Friendly's. You need ice cream—a Jim Dandy Sundae."

I take his hand and Marty pulls me to my feet. He's so strong that I nearly smack into his chest. I stand there for a second. Our eyes are locked and I know how hard it must be for him. I couldn't be around Sean and listen to him bear his soul about someone else. I'd rather shove splinters into my eyes. He remains close, looking down at me with his soft brown eyes. "Thank you for helping me."

"Anytime." Marty's gaze remains locked on my face for a breath longer, and then he turns away.

CHAPTER 11

After Marty dresses in his hippie attire, we head back to my room. I need to grab clothes and shower. "I shouldn't be here. Someone took a shot at me the other day."

By the time I say it, we're already in my room. Amber's been here and dumped half her closet onto my bed. She totally trashed the room and it still smells like smoke. Her bed sheets are rumpled and there's a watermark on them—still fresh. She's so disgusting. I take all of her crap and dump it on her bed.

"I wish she'd keep her crap on her side of the room. I hate it when she does this."

Marty grabs my elbow. I wince and he releases me. The wound still hurts. "What the fuck is going on with you? Who took a shot at you?"

I shake my head. "Not now. Let me get my stuff and get out. If Sean or Black finds out I was here, well, I'd just rather not."

Marty stiffens, and folds his arms across his chest. He looks like a hippie that could take out Manhattan. Irony. "Fine. Hurry up. I'll watch the door, and it goes without saying that anyone that messes with you while I'm around dies."

I smile at him. The words are so wrong that it's ridiculous, especially coming out of his mouth. "Got it."

I manage to shower, change, and grab a bag of clothes before taking off again. Marty and I leave the room and that's when we run into Amber.

"Whore," she says as she walks by.

I stop and turn back, "I'm not the one that has come stains all over my sheets. And, oh yeah, don't throw your crap on my bed. I took the liberty of putting your stuff back on your side of the room. You might want to move that silk slut shirt you like so much. It would be a pity if it got wet."

Marty looks bored. "Seriously? You two are going to have another cat fight? We should buy you both Catwoman costumes. At least that'd be more entertaining."

"Shut up, queer," Amber snaps at him. Marty just laughs in response, which makes Amber turn to nuclear bitch mode. "Laugh it up, because while you two were out talking about boy problems, I was in there actually fucking a real man."

"I think you meant three or forty." Marty replies with a grin on his face. "I forget how whorey you are when we don't see each other for a few days. You see, me, I'm a one guy kinda girl and so is Avery. We're romantics and you're disgusting. Like she said, silk shirt, bottom of the pile of shit Avery tossed on your bed. Better go get it."

"I'm going to get even with you for that, you skank!"

People are watching us now. A few doors have opened and some students mill at the end of the halls. "Go ahead and try." I turn away to leave, but Amber laughs that horrible cackle of hers which makes me turn back.

She's holding up her phone. "Who wants to see Avery sexting with my man?"

For a second, I think she's bluffing, but she turns the volume up on her phone and I hear my voice mid-rapture. I lunge, trying to take the phone from her, but she's already passed it to someone else. Amber gives me a satisfied smile. "Who's the real whore here, Avery? At least I didn't take money from him."

She knows. Holy shit, she knows what I've done.

Amber giggles and shouts at the crowd, "Make sure you have a good look. You can get that kind of action too, and from what I hear, she doesn't cost much." Amber turns back to me and winks. She walks to our room, cackling.

My hands are clenched by my sides and my entire body is shaking. If I go after the phone, they'll play keep-away. I start shaking. Gnashing my teeth together, I hiss, "I hope she dies. She's a horrible excuse for a human being. You goddamn skank!" I scream at her, but Amber is long gone.

Marty's hands are on my shoulders, "Come on, Avery. Walk away."

Tears are streaking down my face. "They're going to share it. That video will be everywhere."

"Knowing Amber, it already is. Walk away. Come on." He tugs my good arm and pulls me down the stairwell. I don't focus on anything until we're in front of the restaurant.

Marty is sitting across from me and I'm slumped back into the seat, hating myself. "This is why I don't think you should take the madam job. If this happened to Black--"

"This wouldn't have happened to Black."

"My point exactly. Sex is power, Avery. Everyone knows that. It's not like Amber got into your private life. If you're going to do this you need to be fearsome. You're not."

I groan, okay, it's more like a whine. "I don't know how."

"Yes, you do. You fight back, and I could tell you wanted to claw her face off. Dial that down a notch so it's not clear how you'll hurt her, but so that she knows it's coming. Then own it. If you fucked half of

Manhattan, own it. Be proud. You chose this life."

Those last three words do something to me. I don't know if it's good or bad, but I feel something combust within me. I'm sick of fighting with people and I crave the respect that Miss Black demands. Maybe I won't be like my mother and make the best meatballs, but who cares when no one respects me?

My gaze drifts up to Marty's. "I did, and I will. No more hiding. No more half-assed Avery."

"Bring it."

"I will, and I won't get even with Amber, I'll own her." A smile snakes across my lips.

"Now, there's my girl."

CHAPTER 12

Marty and I are the only one's ordering ice cream. It isn't even lunchtime yet. I have forbidden chocolate ice cream with peanut butter sauce and hot fudge. Five scoops. Marty is sitting across from me, trying to show me that he can swallow an entire banana.

"And that would impress a woman, because?" I laugh at him when he chokes. "Give me that." I take the other banana half from his ice cream and slip it between my lips until all but the very tip disappears.

"Overachiever."

The way he says it makes me laugh and I start choking. Half the banana goes down and the other half gets chomped off, falls from my mouth, and rolls across the table. Marty's eyes go wide. "That was truly frightening. My junk just jumped up into my body and I doubt it'll come down again for weeks."

I'm laughing and choking. I grab my glass of milk and wash it down. "Your boys need some attention."

"Not from you. Dear God! You chopped it off!"

We're both giggling so much that we can't really speak. When I catch my breath, I manage, "Seriously, Marty. You need to get some action. Date someone. Have a one-nighter."

He offers me a classic Marty look, with the corner of his mouth tugged up into an Elvis-like smile. "Oh, do you have someone in mind? And what are you charging, Miss Thang? Is that going to be your madam name? Because I totally think it should be. Miss Thang, plus some air snaps." He does it and watches me.

I poke at my ice cream. "I'm so torn. I want the white picket fence, not an office full of pricks buying girls."

"So, have both. You can be the suburban madam. Who said you couldn't have the fence?"

Glancing up at him, I answer, "They don't go together. That kind of life is sweet and quiet with kids and a dog. The life Black is offering is flash, power, and cash."

"Like I said, do both." I'm about to tell him that I can't, and he cuts me off. "Think long term, Avery. Do this for a little while, enough to get your house and the life you want, and then quit."

"That sounds familiar."

"You weren't a madam this time and you had a run of bad luck."

"No one would marry me after that. That's a closet and a half full of skeletons, skeletons in the basement, skeletons in the trunk—they'll be everywhere by then." Not to mention the real one decomposing as we speak. The thought makes me nauseous.

I must have turned green, because Marty shoves me his soda. "Drink." After a moment, he asks, "Feel better?"

I nod. "Yeah, thank you."

Leaning back in the booth, Marty nods. "And if it's not too forward, I would."

"I couldn't ask you to do that." I shove ice cream into my mouth and concentrate on the chocolate. The fudgy goodness could make a person orgasmic. A person, being me. I nearly moan.

Marty laughs. "I'd give you a jar of hot fudge every day."

"And I'd be three hundred pounds."

"And I'd never forget your birthday, and I'd occasionally dress like a cowboy just for kicks."

That makes me spew. "Marty!" Sexy cowboy Marty was the funniest thing I'd ever seen and I would have laughed if I didn't want to kill him at the time.

He pushes a napkin at me and wipes my sputtered chocolate spittle off his hands. "I'm serious. I'll be your backup plan. If you say yes to Black, I'll take you no matter how many things you've done—or who you've done. Tell me I'm good enough to be Plan B, Avery. I'll get you the white picket fence and we can name the dog Bob. What do you say?" He holds out his hand, like his offer is serious.

That's when I realize it is. He wants me anyway he can take me, and if I go through with Black's job no one will want me. It'll mean that I've left Sean, because if I chose Black over him, he'll never forgive me.

Reaching out, I take Marty's hand and shake. "Deal. I'm your picket fence wife. When everything turns to shit, you'll sweep me off my feet."

He smiles and follows it up with a wink. "You know it."

CHAPTER 13

I spend the rest of the day hanging out with Marty. My phone rings right after we eat dinner. It's Black. "Hello?"

"Go to your dorm room and wait. Ferro will be there shortly." The line goes dead.

I sigh, and slump back into my seat before pushing my hair out of my face. "Can you drop me back off at the dorm?"

Marty looks confused. "I thought you were supposed to stay away from there."

"I am, but Black said Sean will be there."

Marty nods and pays the tab. He drops me off at the tower and drives away after I go inside. I stand at the bottom of the stairwell, not wanting to face all the jeers that will come when I go up. I decide to grab a drink first and then go up with Sean.

I push through the door and walk to the nearest bar, which is a bit of hike. Cars zoom past me and I worry that each one will try to put a hole in my head. I text Sean and tell him where to meet me.

He replies: *No. Go to your room.*

That makes me laugh. I text back: *Make me.*

Then I pocket my phone and don't answer when he calls. Yes, I'm acting like a petulant child, but he can deal with it. I shove inside and go to a back corner so no one can walk behind me.

The waiter is really hot. He takes my order and brings it right over. "Rough day?" he asks after setting down the vodka in front of me.

"Rough life. Bring a few more of those in a moment."

Hot guy smiles at me. "Yes, ma'am."

I down the drink and only gag a little bit. By the time my third drink is in hand, Sean is in the doorway. He looks pissed and beautiful. His shoulders are squared and his jaw is locked. A dark shirt clings to his chest beneath the leather jacket he loves so much. Blue jeans fit snuggly to his hips and he has on his shit-kicker boots.

Sean glances around the room until he sees me. He takes a few long strides, pulls out a chair, and sits down. "Make me?"

My eyes cut over to Sean. "That's what I said."

"Listen, you can hate me all you want tomorrow. We have this set up. I have a box to sneak you out with, but people need to see you walk into the room. Black's men are in place. You go in and come out. Nothing bad will happen to you. I promise." Sean takes my hands when he says the last two words. "We have to do this."

I nod slowly and finally feel the effects of the alcohol. "I know, but I'm not doing it sober. Claustrophobic girls don't belong in boxes, not unless they're tanked. So here we go." I knock back another drink and accidentally breathe wrong which makes my nose feel like it's caught fire. I choke and reach for my glass of water.

"Lightweight."

"Much better than being a fat whore. A skinny one is preferable, right? *Salute.*" I hold up my next shot glass to him as he gives me a quizzical look.

"What are you talking about?"

"The videos of me sexting Naked Guy. It turns out that Amber didn't delete all of them and this morning she passed around her phone to half the floor and I got to stand there while she did it."

Wrath blazes in Sean's eyes. He stands abruptly and takes my wrist. "Let's go. We'll handle this."

I pull away. "Fuck, no. I'll handle this. I'm going to kick her ass and throw her out the window. Then, I'll climb into my box and let your people clean up the mess." I down another drink before he can pull me away, but most of it spills on the floor. "Sean," I whine his name before dropping the glass on the floor.

The waiter starts to say something. He walks over in front of Sean, but Sean shoves two hundred bucks in his hand. "Sorry about the mess."

Hot waiter guy asks, "Are you all right?"

"Yes, this is Mr. Ferro and Mr. Ferro is sort of grumpy, one hundred percent of the time." I smile at the waiter and wave with my fingertips. "Please excuse me. I need to go find my box."

Sean huffs and waits to scold me until we're outside, but I'm already tipsy, so I don't care. There's a serene smile plastered to my face. "Avery, we're very late. This plan doesn't work if people don't see you."

"Yes, I'm aware." Sean is pissed but he doesn't say anything else. I climb into his little black sports car that's parked at the curb, and we drive back to the dorm. "Where's your bike?"

"I don't ride it anymore."

"Why?"

"Because it's only fun when you're with me. Otherwise it's an oversized, bulky piece of shit."

I giggle. I can't help it. "That's not nice, Sean. You said you liked it. It's so pretty and shiny."

"And heavy and slow…"

Sean drives us back to the dorm and parks toward the back of the lot before he cuts the engine, and comes around to open my door. I can walk but my head feels tingly, which is good. I need to punch Amber in the face and climb in a box. One and two. Sean will get rid of the lunatic that's hunting me and then it'll be fine.

Everything will be fine.

CHAPTER 14

No one says a word to me when Sean's at my side. He's got that scary vibe radiating from him in ginormous waves. We walk up the stairs slowly. Sean is so irritated with me that he's ready to burst. We're very, very late. I didn't bother to tell him which bar I was in exactly, just that it was on Sunrise Highway. So by the time he's found me and gotten me back to the dorm, nearly an hour has passed.

We walk down the hallway together and I wave at people who want to hire me out, but they look afraid of the strong scary man on my arm. I pass Asia's room and see her sitting with her boyfriend. She calls out, "Hey! Avery, wait a sec!" Asia rushes out and gives Sean a look. She's still mad at me, but she doesn't say anything about how I treated her the other day. "I think you're a bitch, but I just found out that Mel ditched all of her finals, which isn't like her at all. If she doesn't come home soon, I'm going to report her missing."

Sean speaks for me. "Your friend hooked up with a rock star and was last sighted about twenty miles from here."

Asia looks shocked. "You saw her?"

"She'll be back shortly. If you'll excuse us, we need to get this girl to bed. She's had a little too much to drink."

"Yeah, sure." Asia disappears into her room.

When we're in front of my door, I can hear Amber is blaring music inside. "Oh gross. That's Amber's doing it song."

"She has a guy in there?" Sean looks down at me, while still holding my arm.

"Yeah, either that or she's doing herself. Amber!" I unlock the door and go inside ready to fight, but all the air is sucked from my lungs. The first thing I see is my roommate sitting on the floor, opposite the door, with a bullet hole in her head. Blood flows from the wound and trails between her eyes. My feet won't move. I can't make them. Sean pushes me inside and utters a slew of swear words, but all I can think is that I wanted her dead and now she is.

My hands fly to my mouth as I try to swallow a sob. That's when I turn slowly and glance at Sean. He's looking around the room, and taking in the pile of crap on Amber's bed. My bedding is half on the floor and half covering my mattress. It's lumpy, like someone is under the sheets. A pink splotch is spreading across my white linens. Sean reaches for the blanket and pulls it back.

Naked Guy is lying in my bed. He was shot several times, but the places that stand out are his shoulders and between his legs. It's like someone wanted to torture him before he died.

That's when I start stuttering, "But that was supposed to be me. That's my bed. Someone wanted to... to do that to me. That was supposed to be me." My body is frigid and I feel like I'm going to hurl.

Sean doesn't wait. He rushes me out of the room and down the stairs and into a car that's waiting. Gabe sounds annoyed, "No box again? Black is going to be—"

"Get her the fuck out of here and don't let her come back. He was already here and mistook her roommate for Avery."

THE ARRANGEMENT VOL 15

To ensure you don't miss the next installment, text AWESOMEBOOKS (one word) to 22828 and you will get an email reminder on release day.

*****

THE FERRO BROTHER MOVIE

Vote now to make it happen!
http://www.ipetitions.com/petition/ferro/

*****

This is a fan driven series-when fans ask for more, there's more.

Go to Facebook and join the discussion!

*****

COMING SOON

BROKEN PROMISES

A Trystan Scott Novel

READ MORE ABOUT CHARACTERS IN THIS BOOK:

BRYAN FERRO

~THE PROPOSITION~

*****

SEAN FERRO

~THE ARRANGEMENT~

******

PETER FERRO GRANZ

~DAMAGED~

******

JONATHAN FERRO

~STRIPPED~

******

TRYSTAN SCOTT

~COLLIDE~

MORE ROMANCE BOOKS BY H.M. WARD:

DAMAGED

DAMAGED 2

STRIPPED

SCANDALOUS

SCANDALOUS 2

SECRETS

THE SECRET LIFE OF
TRYSTAN SCOTT

And more.

To see a full book list, please visit:

www.SexyAwesomeBooks.com/books.htm

CAN'T WAIT FOR H.M WARD'S NEXT STEAMY BOOK?

⭐⭐⭐⭐⭐

Let her know by leaving stars and telling her what you liked about

THE ARRANGEMENT VOL. 14

in a review!

[2]

CPSIA information can be obtained at www.ICGtesting.com
Printed in the USA
LVOW13s1610090414

381019LV00001B/28/P

9 781630 350192